This Boxer Book belongs to

. . . . . . . . . . . . . . . . . . . . . . . . . . . . .

BOXER
BOOKS

www.boxerbooks.com

Boxer® is a registered trademark of Boxer Books Limited.

To all the cats I have ever had the pleasure to know,
fat or otherwise.
J.A.

First published in hardback in Great Britain in 2014 by Boxer Books Limited.
First published in paperback in Great Britain in 2015 by Boxer Books Limited.

www.boxerbooks.com

Boxer®is a registered trademark of Boxer Books Limited.
Text and illustrations copyright © 2014 Jonathan Allen

The right of Jonathan Allen to be identified as the author
and illustrator of this work has been asserted by him
in accordance with the Copyright, Designs and Patents Act, 1988.

A CIP Catalogue record for this book is available
from the British Library upon request.

The illustrations were prepared digitally by the author.

The text is set in Bang
ISBN 978-1-910126-34-9

3 5 7 9 10 8 6 4

Printed in China

All of our papers are sourced from managed forests
and renewable resources.

# Is that my cat?

Jonathan Allen

Boxer Books

Is that my cat?
It can't be.

My cat is a slim,
sleek pussycat.

Is that my cat?
It can't be.

My cat is a little cat
who leaps in and out
of the cat flap.

Is this my cat?
What happened to the
light little cat I could
pick up with one hand?

Is that my cat?
It can't be.

My cat is a fussy
eater who never
finishes her food.

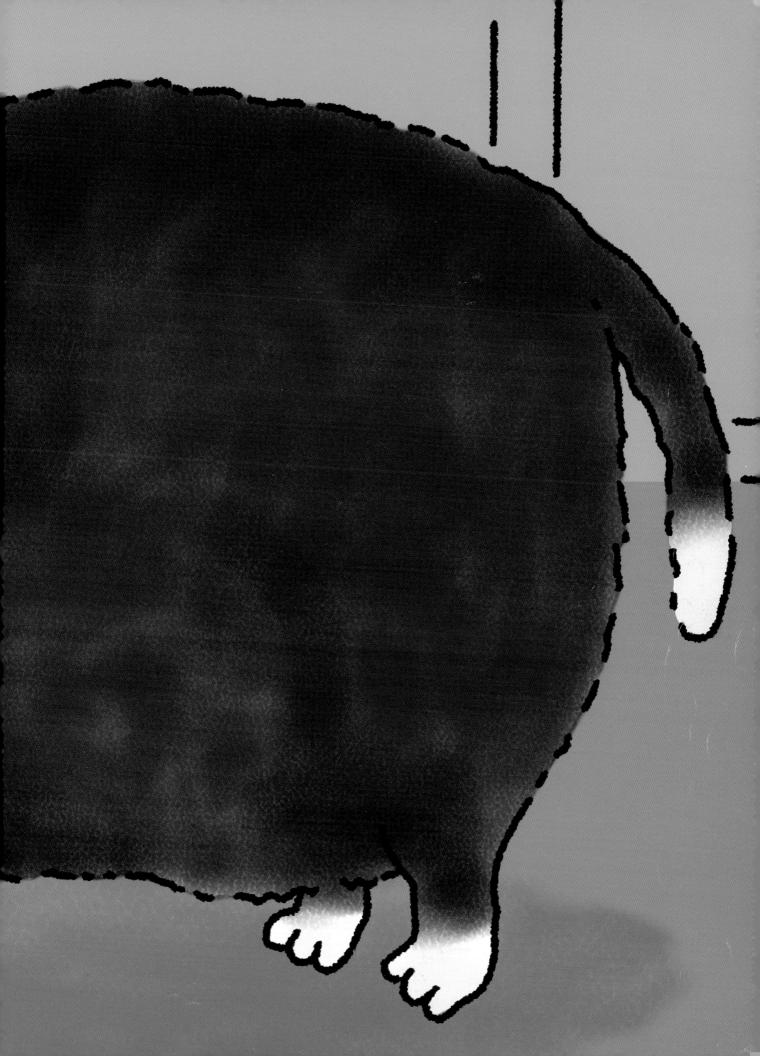

Is that my cat?
No way!
My cat is a mighty
mouse catcher.

Is that my cat?
It can't be.

My cat is a playful puss,
always ready for a game.

That cannot
be my cat.
My cat is a
brave tree
climber.

Is that my cat?
It can't be.
My cat is a wide-awake
cat who sits on the
window sill.

Is that my cat purring in the hall cupboard?

IT IS MY CAT,
and she has kittens.

# Are they my cats?